Bonnie
the Bike-Riding
Fairy

Join the **Rainbow Magic Reading Challenge!**

Read the story and collect your fairy points to climb the
Reading Rainbow at the back of the book.

This book is worth 1 star.

To Tina, who bought me my first bike

Special thanks to
Rachel Elliot

ORCHARD BOOKS

First published in Great Britain in 2019 by The Watts Publishing Group

5 7 9 10 8 6 4

© 2019 Rainbow Magic Limited.
© 2019 HIT Entertainment Limited.
Illustrations © Orchard Books 2019

HIT entertainment

A CIP catalogue record for this book is available from the British Library.

ISBN 978 1 40835 522 0

Printed and bound in Great Britain by Clays Ltd, Elcograf S.p.A

MIX
Paper from
responsible sources
FSC® C104740

FSC
www.fsc.org

The paper and board used in this book are made from wood from responsible sources

Orchard Books
An imprint of Hachette Children's Group
Part of The Watts Publishing Group Limited
Carmelite House, 50 Victoria Embankment, London EC4Y 0DZ

An Hachette UK Company
www.hachette.co.uk
www.hachettechildrens.co.uk

Bonnie
the Bike-Riding
Fairy

By Daisy Meadows

ORCHARD

www.rainbowmagicbooks.co.uk

Jack Frost's Ice Castle

Wetherbury Village

Jack Frost's Spell

I must get strong! I'll start today.
But kids are getting in my way.
They jump and run, they spin and bound.
I can't do sports with them around!

Goblins, ruin every club.
Spoil their sports and make them blub.
I'll prove it's true, for all to see:
My sister's not as strong as me!

Contents

Chapter One: A Boy and a Bell   9

Chapter Two: Collision Course   21

Chapter Three: Riders and Refreshments   29

Chapter Four: Bonnie in a Box   39

Chapter Five: The Castle Raft   49

Chapter Six: A Soggy Goblin   61

Chapter One
A Boy and a Bell

Rachel Walker did ten star jumps and then cartwheeled across the foyer of the Cool Kids Leisure Centre.

"That was so much fun," she said to her best friend, Kirsty Tate.

"Yes, I can't stop smiling," Kirsty said. "I wasn't expecting to enjoy trampolining so much!"

"Thank goodness we were able to help Teri the Trampolining Fairy find her bracelet," said Rachel.

Earlier that day, Teri had whisked them off to Fairyland, where they had met the After-School Sports Fairies. The fairies were very upset because naughty Jack Frost had stolen their magical bracelets. He wanted to get fit so that he could beat his sister Jilly Chilly at arm-wrestling, but he didn't want anyone to see him training. He planned to use the magical bracelets to ruin all after-school sports clubs. Then he would have the leisure centre to himself, where he could train all on his own. Rachel and Kirsty had promised to help return the bracelets to their rightful owners.

"I hope we can find the other bracelets soon," said Rachel. "If all the clubs are as much fun as trampolining, it would be awful if Jack Frost spoiled them."

"Do you want to pick trampolining for our after-school sports club?" Kirsty asked.

"Let's try the other trial classes first,"

said Rachel, laughing. "What's next?"

"There's Lucy," said Kirsty, noticing the young woman who had signed them up for the trial classes. "Let's ask her."

Lucy smiled when she saw them.

"Hi, girls," she said. "You look like you've been enjoying yourselves."

"It was brilliant," said Rachel. "We can't wait to find out what's next."

"How about the bike club?" said Lucy. "You'll find the bike court at the back of the leisure centre. Chris, the cycling teacher, will be there. Have fun!"

Rachel and Kirsty thanked her and skipped outside. As they looked left and right to find which way to go, they saw that there was a wide, sparkling river lined with trees on both sides of the building.

"That's funny," said Rachel. "It must be unusual to have two rivers so close together."

"Oh, my dad told me about this," said Kirsty. "It's not two rivers. It's the river that runs through Wetherbury, and it winds around the leisure centre in a big loop. It flows one way on the east side, and the other way on the west side."

"Then it's like being on an island," said Rachel, smiling. "That sounds exciting. Come on, let's go and find the bike court."

The bike court was behind the main building, in the centre of the river loop. There was a row of gleaming bikes in every colour and size, and a boy in a red cap was practising on a large, tarmacked area. A tall man waved to the girls.

"Welcome to the bike club," he said with a grin. "I'm Chris. Let's get you sorted out with some wheels."

Soon, Rachel and Kirsty were zooming around the bike court while Chris set out some orange cones. Rachel's bike was blue and Kirsty had picked a red one. They stopped beside Chris and he gave

each of them a high five.

"Great riding," he said. "Next, I want you to weave in and out of those cones. This is about learning to control your bike."

Just then, the boy in the red cap pulled his bike up on to its back wheel and wheelied past them.

"Wow, that boy is amazing," said

Rachel. "Did you train him?"

"No, I'm afraid not," said Chris. "He just turned up and started riding."

A new group of children arrived and Chris went to meet them.

"Wheeee!" squealed the boy as he weaved through the cones and spun on his back wheel.

"He's incredible," said Kirsty.

The bike court was starting to get busy.

"Let's go though these cones before it's too crowded," said Rachel.

She pressed her foot down on the pedal . . . and it fell off.

"Oh no," Rachel exclaimed.

THUNK! Kirsty squealed as her seat post collapsed.

"Chris, there's something wrong with my bike," an older girl called out.

Her bike gave a little shudder and the wheels fell off. Rachel and Kirsty gazed around.

"Oh my goodness, I think every single bike is having a problem," said Kirsty.

A chain jammed here, a brake cable snapped there, and one bike toppled over and fell to pieces. Chris was running from one bike to another in a panic.

"Who built these bikes?" he exclaimed. "I've never known anything like it. They're all falling apart."

Soon, there was a pile of broken bikes beside a group of disappointed children. Only one bike was still working.

"Woohoo!" whooped the boy in the red cap.

He did a handstand on his saddle

and waggled his legs in the air. As they waved around, one of his tracksuit legs fell down and showed a flash of green skin. The girls gasped.

"We should have known," Kirsty cried. "He's a goblin!"

"And he's wearing a bracelet," said Rachel, noticing his wrist. "He must be one of the goblins that Jack Frost sent to hide the bracelets. Let's talk to him. He clearly likes this club a lot. Maybe if we explain that he's spoiling it, he'll care enough to give the bracelet back."

She took a step forward and her foot hit something hard.

"Oh, there's a bicycle bell on the ground," she said, looking down at the silvery round shape. "It must have fallen off one of the bikes."

"Or maybe not," said Kirsty.

She picked up the bell and cradled it in her hands. The silver metal was so shiny that it seemed to be glowing.

"It feels warm," Kirsty whispered. "Oh, Rachel, this isn't an ordinary bell. This is magic!"

Chapter Two
Collision Course

DING! The top of the bell opened like a lid, and Bonnie the Bike-Riding Fairy sprang out.

"Hello, Rachel and Kirsty," she said.

The little fairy was wearing a pair of jeans and a dark-blue hooded top with a glittering unicorn on the front.

Her blonde hair was tied back in loose
bunches with little red bows, and her
high-top trainers were sparkling with
silver sequins.

"Bonnie, quickly, hide in my pocket,"
exclaimed Rachel. "We mustn't let
anyone see you."

Bonnie dived into
Rachel's pocket.

"That boy over
there is a goblin,"
Kirsty told her. "We
think he might have
one of the missing
bracelets."

Bonnie peered out
and watched the goblin
riding backwards on his bike.

"I think you're right," she said. "He

must have my bracelet. I have never seen a goblin ride a bike like that. Wow!"

"You sound impressed," said Rachel in surprise.

"I am always impressed when I see someone riding a bike well," said Bonnie. "That doesn't mean he gets to keep my magical bracelet."

"No way," Kirsty agreed.

She ran over to the goblin and stood in front of him. He squeezed his brakes.

"Get out of my way, idiot," he squawked.

"Not until you give back what you stole," said Kirsty.

The goblin pushed his cap up out of his eyes.

"I know you," he said, scowling. "You help the fairies."

"Yes, we do," said Rachel, joining Kirsty. "And we're trying to help them right now. You're having fun on your bike, right? Well, if you give Bonnie's bracelet back, everyone will be able to have as much fun as you."

"I don't care about anyone except me," the goblin yelled. "I want all the fun."

He whirled his bike around and zoomed away from the bike court.

"Come back," Chris called. "You can't take the bike off the leisure centre grounds."

But the goblin had already disappeared among the leafy trees beside the river.

"We'll stop him," Kirsty called to Chris over her shoulder. "Come on, Rachel. We have to catch that goblin."

Bonnie clung on tight as Rachel and

Kirsty sprinted after the goblin. They zigzagged through the trees and darted across winding country lanes, but when they reached a little clearing they had to admit that they had lost him.

"Let's try another way," said Bonnie, flying out of Rachel's pocket.

She waved her wand, and for a second, the world paused. Birds hovered in the air, watching the magic start to work. Golden fairy dust rolled out of the tip of the wand into two fiery circles. The magical hoops rolled around the little clearing and stopped in front of the girls.

"They look like bike wheels," said Kirsty.

The golden circles grew bigger and rose up in front of the girls.

"Step through," said Bonnie.

Rachel and Kirsty each jumped through a hoop. When they landed on the other side, they had become tiny fairies with shimmering gossamer wings.

"Let's find that goblin," said Rachel,

zooming up into the sky.

Fluttering high above the river and fields, it was easy to spot the goblin whizzing along on his bike.

"He's going towards that field," Bonnie said, pointing.

As the fairies flew closer, they saw the goblin lift his bike over a gate and cycle across the middle of a grassy field.

"He shouldn't do that," said Kirsty. "Even if you're allowed into a field, you're supposed to go around the edges. The farmer will get cross."

"Uh-oh," said Rachel. "It's not the farmer that the goblin needs to worry about."

Straight ahead of the goblin, just over the brow of the hill, was a massive bull.

Chapter Three
Riders and Refreshments

"We have to warn him," Bonnie cried.

They swooped down and flew along behind the goblin.

"Stop," they called to him. "Turn back!"

"I'm not listening to a bunch of boring fairies," the goblin yelled. "Go and waggle your wings, you spoilsports – I'm busy having fun."

He zoomed over the brow of the hill,
just as the bull let out a loud snort.

"Argh!" the goblin squawked. "It's a
monster!"

The goblin swerved and tumbled off his bike. The fairies landed beside him.

"It's not a monster, it's an ordinary animal," said Rachel. "Try to stay calm."

Squealing, the goblin scrambled for his bike and leapt into the saddle. He pedalled as fast as he could. The surprised bull turned to watch him go.

"Sorry to disturb you," Kirsty called to the bull.

They zoomed after the goblin. He bumped over the grassy humps, swerved around a cowpat and crashed into a fence. The three fairies landed on the fence, panting.

"Please stop," said Rachel. "We just want to talk to you about the bracelet."

The goblin howled at them. He flung his bike over the fence and sprang after it.

Seconds later he was speeding away from the fairies.

"HEEELLLP!" he squealed, his legs sticking out as he shot down the steep track.

"Here we go again," said Bonnie.

The fairies zoomed after him as he zigzagged down the track. From above, they could see that there were two horse riders further along.

"He's going to crash straight into them," said Bonnie in alarm.

"We need to let those horses know that

they're in danger," said Kirsty.

She and Rachel swooped down towards the horses, one black and one dappled grey. They were walking down the track side by side. Their riders, two teenage girls, were laughing about something that had happened at school. Rachel darted into the ear of the horse on the right, and Kirsty fluttered into the ear of the other horse.

"Please listen, there isn't much time," said Rachel.

"A goblin on a bike is about to crash

into you," Kirsty exclaimed. "Move to the side, quickly!"

The horses twitched their ears and plunged into the hedges at the sides of the track.

"What are you doing, Shadow?"

exclaimed the rider of the black horse.

"Biscuit, stop it," said the other girl.

WHIZZ! The goblin shot between the horses and the riders screamed. Rachel and Kirsty flew up to join Bonnie, and the horses whinnied to say thank you.

"Oh my goodness, well done," said Bonnie. "That could have been a nasty accident."

"We have to stop him soon or there will be an accident," said Rachel. "He's riding as if he's in a bike race."

"That gives me an idea," said Kirsty, clapping her hands together. "In bike competitions, there's always a refreshments stand so the riders can get a drink. Bonnie, could you turn us back into humans and set up a lemonade stand?"

"Great idea," said Bonnie. "We just have to get far enough ahead of him."

Flying as fast as they could, the fairies followed the winding track. They spotted a place where the track grew wider, close beside the river.

"That's perfect," said Rachel.

They landed next to the river, and Bonnie tapped Rachel and Kirsty with her wand. Fairy magic spun them around, growing them to human size in the blink of an eye. Then Bonnie tapped a large boulder. It turned into a candy-striped lemonade stall, with jugs of sparkling, ice-cold lemonade.

"Quick, I can hear him coming," said Rachel.

She darted behind the stall, and Kirsty found herself holding a sign.

Bonnie hid behind the sign. The next moment, the goblin whizzed around a bend in the track and skidded to a halt.

"Give me that lemonade," he demanded.

Rachel poured a cup of lemonade. When he reached out to take it, she noticed that his wrist was bare.

"I heard about a cyclist once who always wears a lucky charm around her neck," she said as he glugged the lemonade. "Do you wear anything to bring you good luck?"

"I sometimes wear a special bracelet," the goblin said.

"Where is it?" Kirsty asked.

The goblin looked at her and narrowed his eyes. Then he jerked his thumb at the pannier box on his bike rack.

"In there," he said.

Rachel poured another cup of lemonade and Kirsty stood in front of the goblin so he couldn't see his bike. Then Bonnie fluttered down to the pannier box.

"Please don't let him turn around," she whispered. "I have to get my bracelet back."

Chapter Four
Bonnie in a Box

"Tell us all about being a cyclist," said Kirsty.

She saw Bonnie tap the pannier box.

"It's very dangerous and exciting," said the goblin in a boastful voice. "I'm the fastest and the best."

The pannier box lid clicked open. The

goblin started to turn around.

"Let me give you some more," said
Rachel.

"I haven't finished this one yet, stupid,"
the goblin snapped.

Bonnie slipped into the pannier box.
Then suddenly, everything happened very
quickly. The goblin threw his lemonade
at Kirsty and whirled around, slamming

his hand down on the
pannier box lid.

"Got you!" he yelled.

Dripping with icy
lemonade, Kirsty tried to
grab at him. He ducked
away from her and
jumped on his bike.

"Jack Frost warned
me that you would try
to get my bracelet," he
jeered.

He pulled up his sleeve, and the girls
saw Bonnie's shining bracelet around his
upper arm. He pushed it back down to
his wrist.

"Ha ha, tricked you," he said in a sing-
song voice. "Now I've got a magical
bracelet and a fairy. I'm going to be Jack

Frost's Goblin of the Month for sure."

He blew a loud raspberry at them and then pedalled away at top speed. In seconds he was out of sight.

"What are we going to do?" cried Rachel. "Bonnie's trapped in that pannier box. We have to save her."

"We're not fast enough to catch him on foot," said Kirsty, squeezing lemonade out of her hair.

"Maybe we should use our magical lockets to go to Fairyland," said Rachel. "We could find help there."

Queen Titania had given each of them a locket with a pinch of fairy dust inside. They knew that if they were ever in trouble, they could use it to reach Fairyland. Rachel put her hand on her locket and then paused.

"Listen," she said. "I can hear voices."

Kirsty paused too, her head on one side.

"Me too," she said. "I can hear laughter and splashing."

"The river!" Rachel exclaimed.

They hopped from boulder to boulder until they were standing on the very edge of the water. Coming around the bend in the river was a straggling line of very, very strange rafts.

"That one looks like a dragon," said Rachel, pointing to a green one with a head that was breathing fake fire.

"There's one that's just two barrels roped together," Kirsty exclaimed.

There were rafts in the shape of cars, rafts made to look like animals and rafts with sails. There was one that looked like a Viking longship and even a shark raft with teeth. Some people were paddling with their hands and others had oars shaped like webbed feet, and they were all rushing down the river towards the girls.

"I know what this is," Kirsty exclaimed. "It's the annual Wetherbury Raft Race.

Every year, people make the funniest, craziest rafts and try to sail them all the way from Wetherbury Bridge to the big weir. Anyone can enter the competition, but they are only allowed to use certain

things to make the rafts. It always looks
like a lot of fun."

"Kirsty, this is our chance to catch up
with the goblin," said Rachel suddenly.
"When we were fairies, I saw that the
track stays close to the river."

"Yes," said Kirsty, "and the river loops
back on itself close to the leisure centre,
remember? That's why we could see the
river on both sides of the bike court."

"If we were on one of those rafts, we
might be able to catch up with him at a
bridge where he has to cross the river,"
said Rachel.

"But how do we get on board one of
the rafts?" Kirsty asked. "We're not fairies
any more, so we can't fly."

"We don't have to fly," said Rachel.
"We can jump."

Kirsty stared at her best friend in surprise.

"That sounds a bit scary," she said. "Are you sure?"

"The water just in front of us is calm," said Rachel. "It's the best place to jump, and we've both just done lots of jumping practice in the trampolining club. We can do it. Besides, Bonnie's in trouble and she needs us. It's worth taking a bit of a risk to help a friend."

"You're right," said Kirsty. "Look, the rafts are close now. Get ready!"

Chapter Five
The Castle Raft

Holding hands, Rachel and Kirsty
leapt from the biggest boulder. They
landed with a bump on a castle-shaped
raft called the *Mary Sue*. There were
two teenage boys on board, dressed as
knights, and they stared at the girls in
amazement.

"Hey, what are you doing?" cried the black-haired boy.

"You can't be on board," said the brown-haired boy. "We haven't got enough oars to go round."

"Please," said Rachel, clinging on as the raft was tossed around on the foaming water. "We're following someone who has stolen something from our friend. He's on a bike and we can't catch up with him if we run. But on this raft we might just have a chance. Please help us."

The boys exchanged a quick glance. Then they nodded and held out their hands.

"I'm Tom and this is Alex," said the black-haired boy. "Welcome aboard the *Mary Sue*."

"And hold on tight," added Alex. "It's

going to be a bumpy ride."

At that moment, the *Mary Sue* plunged into the next, fast-flowing section of the river. Tons of rushing water carried them past the trees and boulders that lined the riverbanks. Another raft jerked past them, laden with eight paddlers and decorated with flowery bunting.

"Let's overtake them!" shouted Tom.

The boys had screwed handles to the deck, and the girls grabbed them and clung on tightly. Water sprayed over them, and in seconds both Rachel and Kirsty were drenched.

"There's a good bit coming up," Alex yelled, wiping his face.

The girls squealed with excitement as the raft zigzagged around jagged boulders.

"This is like the most amazing fairground ride ever," shouted Rachel.

The raft slowed down and the girls had a chance to look around.

"Phew, another quiet stretch of river," said Tom. "It gives us a quick rest."

"And a chance to look around," said Kirsty.

She checked the riverbanks, but there was no sign of the goblin. Then she looked up at the bridge ahead and gasped.

"There he is," she cried out.

The goblin heard her as he pedalled across the bridge. The girls saw his expression change from happy to horrified.

"Come back," Rachel called out to him.

"No way," the goblin yelled back. He zoomed off the bridge and the track disappeared among the trees. At the same time, the raft started to gather speed.

"Oh my goodness, poor Bonnie must be being bumped around terribly," said Kirsty. "Where will we see the track next, Alex?"

Still paddling with one hand, Alex

checked his map.

"There's another quiet bit coming up soon," he said. "There's a bridge there too. Maybe we'll spot him there."

The rafts stuck close together, and the sound of cheers and whoops made the girls want to join in. They cheered whenever the *Mary Sue* inched ahead of another raft, and booed whenever it got overtaken. Every now and then they glimpsed the goblin, crossing bridges or wobbling along the riverside track. But they were never close enough, or going slowly enough, to jump off the raft.

"Rachel, what will we do if we can't get off the raft?" Kirsty asked. "We might have to ride this all the way to Wetherbury. I don't think my dad will be very happy if I go home without him."

"I don't think we need to worry," said Rachel, pointing ahead.

Straight ahead, the river grew wider and calmer. The raft drifted closer to the bank.

"This part of the river is quite deep and calm, and the current is gentle," said Tom. "It slows all the rafts down."

Kirsty stood up and pointed at a building ahead.

"That's the Cool Kids Leisure Centre," she said. "We're almost back where we started from."

"And we're ahead of the goblin," Rachel added. "Let's get off the raft and see if we can stop him here."

Tom and Alex paddled the raft close to the bank, and the girls jumped into the long grasses.

"Thank you," they called, waving as the castle raft floated on down the river. "Good luck!"

"Goodbye!" called the boys.

Rachel and Kirsty scrambled out of the bushes and found themselves standing on the track. There were tall grasses on either side.

"The goblin will have to stop when he sees us," said Kirsty.

"There he is!" Rachel exclaimed.

The goblin came whizzing around the bend and saw the girls.

"Out of my way," he yelled. "Move!"

"Not without Bonnie," Kirsty called out.

Holding hands, the girls stood still as

the bike zoomed towards them.

"He's not slowing down," Rachel said.

Kirsty squeezed her hand.

"He will," she whispered. "He must!"

Chapter Six
A Soggy Goblin

With a yell, the goblin swerved and rode straight into the tall grasses beside the river. His bike jerked to a stop, and he flew over the handlebars.

"Yikes!" he squawked.

There was an almighty *SPLASH!* The girls pushed through the grasses and saw the goblin flailing around in the water.

"I can't swim," he spluttered, spitting out river water. "Get me out of here!"

The girls lay on their tummies and reached out their hands to the goblin. His arms waved wildly.

"Calm down," said Rachel. "Just reach for our hands."

The goblin was panicking too much to listen, but the girls managed to grip his wrists and pull him out of the water. As soon as he was on dry land, he shook their hands off.

"Let go of me," he snapped. "This is all your fault."

"None of this would have happened if you hadn't stolen a bracelet and fairy-napped Bonnie," said Kirsty.

She knelt down beside the bike and opened the pannier box. Bonnie fluttered out.

"Bonnie, are you OK?" Rachel asked, kneeling down next to Kirsty.

"I'm fine," Bonnie said, smiling. "Just a bit crumpled! Thank you for rescuing me. How did you do it?"

Quickly, the girls told her about the raft race and the kind boys who had given them a lift.

"I wish I had seen the goblin's face when he realised you were ahead of him," said Bonnie with a laugh.

"Oh, where is the goblin?" Rachel exclaimed.

The girls jumped up and saw the goblin squelching away from them down the track.

"We have to stop him," said Rachel. "Bonnie, he still has your bracelet."

"Oh no, he doesn't," said Kirsty with a smile.

She opened her hand and showed Rachel and Bonnie a shining bracelet.

"Yes!" cheered Bonnie,

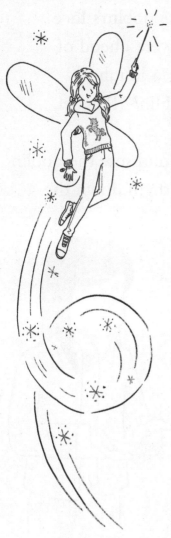

twirling into the air. "My magical bracelet!"

"But how did you get it?" asked Rachel, turning to Kirsty in astonishment.

"It happened when we were pulling him out of the water," Kirsty explained. "His wrist was so slippery that it just slid right off into my hand. I don't think he even noticed."

Bonnie put her hand on the gleaming bracelet, and it shrank

to fairy size at once. She put it on her
wrist and then flew up to kiss each of the
girls on the cheek.

"Thank you," she said. "You're my
heroes."

"We're glad we could help," said Kirsty.

"I must take my bracelet back to Fairyland," said Bonnie. "Thanks to you, cycling clubs all over the world will be able to carry on – including yours."

She vanished in a twinkling of fairy dust, and Rachel picked up the goblin's bike.

"Let's get back to the leisure centre and see what the bike club should really be like," she said.

When Rachel and Kirsty wheeled the bike on to the court, it was filled with riders practising their skills. The girls exchanged a happy smile and Chris gave them a thumbs-up.

"Well done for finding the bike," he said. "But where's the rider?"

"He went home," said Kirsty truthfully. "I think he decided that the bike riding club isn't for him after all."

"At least the bike is in one piece," said Chris.

"It looks as if you got the other bikes working again," said Rachel.

"Yes, the strange thing is that they

weren't broken after all," said Chris. "I took another look at them a few minutes ago and they were fine. I can't understand how I made such a mistake – but I'm very glad I was wrong."

Rachel and Kirsty exchanged a secret smile. They knew that the bikes were working because Bonnie was safely back in Fairyland with her magical bracelet.

"Now, which bikes were yours?" Chris

asked the girls.

Soon, Kirsty was back on her red bike and Rachel was on the blue one.

Rachel leaned closer to her best friend.

"Now there are only two magical bracelets missing," she whispered. "Rita the Rollerskating Fairy and Callie the Climbing Fairy must be so worried. I wonder which of them will come and find us next."

"I'm looking forward to finding out," Kirsty replied.

Just then, Chris beckoned them over to a small ramp at the side of the court.

"How do you two feel about trying some simple jumps on your bikes?" he asked. "I watched you riding earlier and I think you're ready."

Rachel and Kirsty exchanged a smile,

remembering their jumps on and off the raft.

"Let's go for it," said Rachel. "I can do anything when my best friend's along for the ride!"

The End

**Now it's time for Kirsty and
Rachel to help ...**

Rita the Rollerskating Fairy

Read on for a sneak peek ...

"I love the Cool Kids Leisure Centre,"
said Kirsty Tate.

She held out her arms and twirled
around in the middle of the foyer.

"Me too," said her best friend, Rachel
Walker. "I'm so glad it opened halfway
between Tippington and Wetherbury. It's
brilliant that we get to choose an after-
school club together."

Lucy, the lady who was organising the
after-school sports clubs, looked up as
they walked over to her.

"How was the bike club?" she asked.

"It was even more exciting than we

expected," said Kirsty, sharing a secret smile with Rachel.

With the help of Bonnie the Bike-Riding Fairy, Rachel and Kirsty had chased a cycling goblin around the countryside, ridden a raft down a rushing river and rescued Bonnie's magical bracelet. As friends of Fairyland, they were used to enchanted adventures. But their adventure with Bonnie had been one of the most exciting yet.

"I'm very glad to hear that you had fun at the bike club," said Lucy. "There are two other clubs running this afternoon. Would you like to try rollerskating next?"

"That would be great," said Rachel. "I love rollerskating."

"The teacher, Liz, has set up in hall

two," said Lucy. "She'll fit you with a pair of rollerskates."

Rachel and Kirsty thanked her and hurried towards hall two. They opened the door and met a blast of pop music and laughter. Rollerskaters were skidding slowly across the room. Their arms were held out wide and their legs were wobbling.

"Hi, and welcome to Rollerskating Club," said a young woman with long, dark hair. "I'm Liz. I can't wait to get you started. Rollerskating is great fun and a fantastic way to keep fit."

The girls told her their names and she went to get them some skates. Rachel and Kirsty shared a worried look.

"I hope that Jack Frost doesn't cause trouble for this club," said Kirsty. "He's already made the bikes break and the trampolines collapse."

"I keep thinking about that too," said Rachel. "Keep a lookout for goblins."

Jack Frost had stolen four of the magical bracelets that belonged to the After-School Sports Fairies.

Read Rita the Rollerskating Fairy to find out what adventures are in store for Kirsty and Rachel!

Read the brand-new series from Daisy Meadows...

Unicorn Magic™

Ride. Dream. Believe.

Meet best friends Aisha and Emily and journey to the secret world of Unicorn Valley!

Calling all parents, carers and teachers!
The Rainbow Magic fairies are here to help
your child enter the magical world of reading.
Whatever reading stage they are at, there's
a Rainbow Magic book for everyone!
Here is Lydia the Reading Fairy's guide to
supporting your child's journey at all levels.

Starting Out

Our Rainbow Magic Beginner Readers are perfect for first-time readers who are just beginning to develop reading skills and confidence. Approved by teachers, they contain a full range of educational levelling, as well as lively full-colour illustrations.

①

Developing Readers

Rainbow Magic Early Readers contain longer stories and wider vocabulary for building stamina and growing confidence. These are adaptations of our most popular Rainbow Magic stories, specially developed for younger readers in conjunction with an Early Years reading consultant, with full-colour illustrations.

②

Going Solo

The Rainbow Magic chapter books – a mixture of series and one-off specials – contain accessible writing to encourage your child to venture into reading independently. These highly collectible and much-loved magical stories inspire a love of reading to last a lifetime.

③

www.rainbowmagicbooks.co.uk

"Rainbow Magic got my daughter reading chapter books. Great sparkly covers, cute fairies and traditional stories full of magic that she found impossible to put down" - Mother of Edie (6 years)

"Florence LOVES the Rainbow Magic books. She really enjoys reading now" - Mother of Florence (6 years)

Read along the Reading Rainbow!

Well done – you have completed the book!

This book was worth 1 star.

See how far you have climbed on the Reading Rainbow opposite.
The more books you read, the more stars you can colour in
and the closer you will be to becoming a Royal Fairy!

Do you want to print your own Reading Rainbow?

1) Go to the Rainbow Magic website

2) Download and print out the poster

3) Colour in a star for every book you finish
and climb the Reading Rainbow

4) For every step up the rainbow,
you can download your very own certificate

There's all this and lots more at
rainbowmagicbooks.co.uk

You'll find activities, stories, a special newsletter
AND you can search for the fairy with your name!